D0455597

BENNY AND PENNY
IN
THE TOY BREAKER

A TOON BOOK BY

GEOFFREY HAYES

A JUNIOR LIBRARY GUILD SELECTION

BANK STREET COLLEGE OF EDUCATION

Best Children's Books of the Year

KIRKUS BEST OF '09 CONTINUING SERIES

For Leigh Stein,
who is Penny in disguise

Editorial Director: FRANÇOISE MOULY

Book Design: FRANÇOISE MOULY & JONATHAN BENNETT

GEOFFREY HAYES' artwork was drawn in colored pencil.

 All our books are Smyth Sewn (the highest library-quality binding available) and printed wi soy-based inks on acid-free, woodfree paper harvested from responsible sources. Printed in Malaysia by Tien Wah Press. Distributed to the trade by Consortium Book Sales; orders (800) 283-3572; orderentry@perseusbooks.com; www.cbsd.co
The Library of Congress has cataloged the hardcover edition as follows:
Hayes, Geoffrey. Benny and Penny in the toy breaker : a TOON Book / by Geoffrey Hayes. p. cm.
Summary: When their cousin Bo comes to visit, Benny and Penny hide their toys and try to go on a treasure hunt witho him, but Bo will not stop pestering them. ISBN: 978-1-935179-07-8 (hardcover)
1. Graphic novels. [1. Graphic novels. 2. Bullies–Fiction. 3. Brothers and sisters–Fiction. 4. Cousins–Fiction. 5. Mice–Fiction.] I. Title.
Title: Toy breaker. PZ7.7.H39Bdm 2010 [E]–dc22 2009038066
ISBN: 978-1-935179-28-3
15 16 17 18 19 20 TWP 7 6 5 4 3 2

www.TOON-BOOKS.com

BENNY and PENNY

in

"THE TOY BREAKER"

Benny?

What's "LOOT"?
Loot is treasure-*gold!*
I have spoons to dig with...
A pail to
dirt in...
And a spyglass to look for clues.
TREE
START
LOOT
BENNY'S MAP

Benny...Penny!
Cousin Bo is here.

BO?!

h no!
BO!

Quick!
Hide all the
toys!

Bo always
BREAKS
them!

HEY!
What are you guys doing?
Oh, nothing!
Me too!
Where are all your toys?
Mommy took them to be ***cleaned.***
HA! HA!
You're funny!
Monkey can't play today. He's ***sick.***
No, he's not!
He's just a ***doll!***
!

There's a toy!

Don't!

I have one of these. Watch!

I can do ***this...***

And I can do ***this...***

And ***this!***

BONK!

GIVE THAT TO ME!!
RAZZ!
You'll break it!
I will *not!*
BONK!
Say, what's this?

You can't look!
That's a **SECRET**!
A secret what?
A secret *pirate map!*
We're hunting for *loot!*
We are?

Not you, ***us!***
But I'm good at finding stuff!

Watch...
It's ***not*** in the sandbox!

SNATCH!
Thanks for telling me!

O-HO-HEE!
SPLASH!
It's pirate loot for me!
That's ***our*** map!
Give it back!
I'm going to tell!

OH! Are you going to tell your ***mommy?***

HA! HA! HA! HA!

BOOM!

I got it!

Good work!

There you are!
Where is the map?
It must be lost.
We don't have it.
Nope!

Oh, I don't care!

I'm going to play on the slide!

Good! Now **we** can look for the loot!

Oh boy!

One...
Two...

One!
Two!

I will count!
Okay.

One...
Two... Three... Four... Five!

STOP THAT!

Or what? Are you going to cry for *mommy*?

Now, we have to find a ***tree!***

Here is a tree!

And ***here*** is a tree!

SHHH! Now we have to find an *arrow!*
An arrow.
An arrow.
Here is one!
THIS END UP
You are **NOT** playing!

Then I will play with Monkey.
NO!

Leave Monkey alone! He's *sick!*
No, he's not!

RIP!!

Well... Maybe he *is!*
GAAAAA!!

YOU BROKE MONKEY!!!

Why can't you ever play **NICE**?
He's just a ***doll***!
Poor Monkey!
Mommy can fix him.
Just ask her.
kay.
They don't want to play with me.
I will find some ***other*** kids to play with!
I will show them!

I'm stuck!

MOMMY!
Bo?

Penny, Bo is just trying to fool us!

HELP

What's wrong?

He's ***stuck!***

I am ***not!***

If you went in, you can go back out.

STOP IT!

YEOW!!

You can do it!
We'll help you, Bo.
Okay.

Now...
One...
Two...

hree!
POP!

Are you all right?
I think so...
Here. I saved his cap.
Thanks.
LOOK!
Hey bird, let go of that!

Oh **NO**!
Now the ***bird*** will find the loot!

It's ***gone!***
Now you ***really*** won't want to play with me.
Yes we will...
...***if*** you don't break things.
I'm sorry I broke Monkey.
But what can we play with ***no*** map?

HMMMMM
Oh, who needs an old map to find loot?
Who needs loot?
THIS END UP
Who needs toys?
We'll just play!
Then nothing can get broken!

Tee-hee!
WOW!
Look what I found!
Hey! We were playing!
I have something to do first.
PENNY!
MONKEY!

Here, Penny. I made this for Monkey.
GET WELL MONKEY
LOVE BO!
Thanks, Bo. Monkey feels **better** now.
So do ***I***.
Me ***too***!
THE END

ABOUT THE AUTHOR

Geoffrey Hayes is the author/illustrator of the Patrick Brown books and of the extremely successful series of early readers Otto and Uncle Tooth. His best-selling TOON Books series, Benny and Penny, has garnered multiple awards. *Benny and Penny in The Big No-No!* won the 2010 Theodor Seuss Geisel Award, given to "the most distinguished American book for beginning readers published during the preceding year." He lives and works in New York City.